This book belongs to:

_____

For my wife, Ginger, who revived it,

my children, Rob and Jennifer, who encouraged it,

and for Denise Cronin, who made it happen.

BRAVE
CHICKEN
LITTLE

Retold and illustrated by **Robert Byrd**

Viking
An Imprint of Penguin Group (USA)

One fine day Mrs. Chicken Licken decided to bake a cake.

But there was nothing to make it with, so she sent Chicken Little

off to the market to buy honey and flour and milk.

"Do not dillydally," she said. "Come straight home."

Chicken Little skipped down the shady country road, and . . .

Whack!

An acorn fell smack on top of his poor little head.

"Owww!" he cried. "The sky is falling! I must go and tell the king!"

Chicken Little ran down the road, where he met Henny Penny.

"The sky is falling!" he cried. "I must go and tell the king."

"Oh, I shall go with you," she said.

Chicken Little and Henny Penny both ran down the road, where
they met Ducky Lucky and Turkey Lurkey.

"Where are you going?" they asked.

"The sky is falling!" cried Chicken Little and Henny Penny.

"And we are going to tell the king."

"Then we shall go, too," they said.

Chicken Little, Henny Penny, Ducky Lucky, and Turkey Lurkey all ran on down the road.

There they met Piggy Wiggy, Rabbit Babbit, and Natty Ratty.

"Where are you running to?" they asked.

"The sky is falling!" cried Chicken Little, Henny Penny, Ducky Lucky, and Turkey Lurkey. "And we are going to tell the king."

"Well, we will go with you," they said.

Now Chicken Little, Henny Penny, Ducky Lucky, Turkey Lurkey, Piggy Wiggy, Rabbit Babbit, and Natty Ratty all ran down the road. And they met Froggy Woggy and Roly and Poly Moley. "Where are you all off to?" they called.

"The sky is falling!" cried Chicken Little, Henny Penny, Ducky Lucky, Turkey Lurkey, Piggy Wiggy, Rabbit Babbit, and Natty Ratty. "And we are going to tell the king."

"Then so shall we!" they cried.

So down the road ran Chicken Little, Henny Penny, Ducky Lucky, Turkey Lurkey, Piggy Wiggy, Rabbit Babbit, Natty Ratty, Froggy Woggy, and Roly and Poly Moley.

And whom should they meet but—Foxy Loxy.

"Hello, hello," he sang out. "Good day and cheers! Where are you off to, my scrumptious little dears?"

"The sky is falling," said Chicken Little. "And we are going to tell the king."

"Oh please, please, let me come, too! I know the best way, I do!
I do!" said Foxy with a grin.

"But first, my dear friends, we'll stop for brunch, or maybe instead,
a nice little lunch.

"And after we eat, we'll dance and we'll sing on our way through
the woods to the palace of the king."

And so, Chicken Little, Henny Penny, Ducky Lucky, Turkey Lurkey, Piggy Wiggy, Rabbit Babbit, Natty Ratty, Froggy Woggy, and Roly and Poly Moley followed the grinning Foxy Loxy down the road, over the hill, and into his house.

"My dears," said Foxy Loxy, "meet my wife, the love of my life."

Mrs. Foxy Loxy smiled and curtsied.

Then Foxy Loxy said, "And these are my kits, who frazzle my wits."

And one by one, Foxy Boxy, Foxy Doxy, Foxy Hoxy, Foxy Moxy,
Foxy Noxy, Foxy Poxy, and Foxy Soxy smiled and licked their lips.

Then Foxy Loxy said, "Come in and stay for awhile. Lunch will be
served in spectacular style!"

"But the water has not quite boiled for our extraordinary stew! And what a surprise is in store for you. . . ."

Foxy Loxy quickly opened a small door and pushed Chicken Little, Henny Penny, Ducky Lucky, Turkey Lurkey, Piggy Wiggy, Rabbit Babbit, Natty Ratty, Froggy Woggy, and Roly and Poly Moley down the steps into a dark and gloomy cellar.

Slam!

And Foxy Loxy locked the door.

Down in the cellar, the animals were bawling and moaning and squalling and groaning.

"Oh what can we do? What can we do?

"We are all about to wind up in the stew!"

"Be quiet," said Chicken Little. "Let us think."

He looked around very carefully and saw a small window, high up on the wall.

"A-ha!" he said.

Everyone looked up at the window.

"Hurry!" Piggy Wiggy cried. "We must climb out!"

They ran to the wall and began to pile on top of each other. Piggy Wiggy first, then Turkey Lurkey and Ducky Lucky. Then Rabbit Babbit.

When Henny Penny climbed up, they began to swing and sway.

When Natty Ratty reached the top, they teetered and tottered, until Turkey Lurkey's feathers tickled poor Piggy Wiggy's nose.

Ahhh! Ahhh!
Ahh-chooo!
The thunderous sneeze
sent everyone crashing into
a heap on the floor.

Chicken Little looked
on in dismay.

"Oh dear," he said.
"This will never do."

"We need to make something to climb that is solid and strong," Chicken Little declared.

He saw that the corner of the cellar was filled with junk.

"Come on!" he cried out. "Help me push this rubble under the window."

Together, the animals took pots and pans, sacks of potatoes, pieces of wood, broken furniture, buckets, barrels, bricks, and baskets and piled them up as high as they could.

"I am the only one who will fit," said Chicken Little.

And up he went. Higher and higher until he reached the top.

"Wait here for me," he called down, and he squeezed through the window.

And whom should he see but—Foxy Loxy.

Chicken Little climbed up a nearby tree to take a closer look.

Very carefully he crawled onto a long branch filled with big, juicy apples.

Bonk!

A low-hanging apple banged his head, which was still sore from the
acorn.

"Hmmm," he thought. He paused for a moment and looked around.

Below him he could see Foxy Loxy sunning himself, waiting for the water to boil.

"I wonder what Chicken Little will do, when he finds himself and his friends in a stew?

"What a foolish thing to say, that the sky is falling down today!"

Whack!

An apple hit Foxy Loxy smack on his head.

"Ahhhh!" he shouted.

Whack!

Chicken Little aimed and bounced another apple off Foxy's head.

"Help!" Foxy Loxy cried. "Oh me, oh my! I've just been hit by a piece of the sky!"

Mrs. Foxy Loxy ran outside and . . .

Whack!

Chicken Little bounced an apple off her head, too.

"Aggggggh!" she shrieked. "The sky is really falling! We must go and tell the king!"

So Foxy Loxy, Mrs. Foxy Loxy, and Foxy Boxy, Foxy Doxy, Foxy Hoxy, Foxy Moxy, Foxy Noxy, Foxy Poxy, and Foxy Soxy all ran off to tell the king that the sky was indeed falling.

Then Brave Chicken Little climbed down the tree and ran inside the house. He unlocked the cellar door and Henny Penny, Ducky Lucky, Turkey Lurkey, Piggy Wiggy, Rabbit Babbit, Natty Ratty, Froggy Woggy, and Roly and Poly Moley all stumbled out, tumbling and tripping, screaming and screeching.

Chicken Little ran out right behind them.

He ran down the road and through the woods as fast as he could.

And whom should he see, out for a stroll, but—the king himself.

But Chicken Little did not stop.

And he did not tell the king that the sky was falling.

He just ran and ran and ran, all the way home.

"Chicken Little!" cried Mrs. Chicken Licken. "Where have you been?"

But Chicken Little was so tired, he did not answer. Soon he was dreaming of baking cakes, ferocious foxes, majestic kings, giant acorns, and falling apples.

And he never, ever did tell anyone else that the sky had fallen.

VIKING
Published by the Penguin Group
Penguin Group (USA) LLC
375 Hudson Street
New York, New York 10014

USA * Canada * UK * Ireland * Australia
New Zealand * India * South Africa * China

penguin.com
A Penguin Random House Company

First published in the United States of America by Viking, an imprint of Penguin Young
Readers Group, 2014

LIBRARY OF CONGRESS CATALOGING-IN-PUBLICATION DATA
Byrd, Robert, author, illustrator.
Brave Chicken Little / retold and illustrated by Robert Byrd.
pages cm
Summary: A retelling of the classic story of Chicken Licken, who has an acorn fall on
his head and runs in a panic to his friends Henny Penny, Ducky Lucky, and others, to tell
them the sky is falling.
ISBN 978-0-670-78616-9 (hardcover)
[1. Folklore.] I. Chicken Licken. II. Title.
PZ8.1.B98Br 2014
398.2—dc23
[E]
2013032616

Manufactured in China

1   2   3   4   5   6   7   8   9   10

Designed by Jim Hoover